BLOOD BENEATH THE SAND

EVAN DAVIES

Copyright © 2023 by Evan Davies

All rights reserved.

No part of this book may be reproduced or transmitted in any form or by any means, electronic or mechanical, except for the purpose of review and/or reference, without explicit permission in writing from the publisher.

Cover design copyright © 2023 by Niki Lenhart
nikilen-designs.com

Published by Water Dragon Publishing
waterdragonpublishing.com

ISBN 978-1-959804-87-1 (Trade Paperback)

FIRST EDITION

10 9 8 7 6 5 4 3 2 1

AUTHOR'S NOTE

I could point you to a number of places where the seed of this story began to germinate. I could talk about inspirations and influences and all those magic things, but the truth is, there was a short story contest called *Fantasy-Noir* that was offering pretty good cash.

I didn't win.

That's the thing about writing though; what you wind up with at the end is never exactly what you had in mind at the start. There's a thing in your head, and after a few hours or days or years, there's a thing on the page, and no matter how good you get at translating one into the other, they're never really the same.

I started writing this story in a pretty cynical headspace, and somewhere along the line, after rejections and rewrites and incalculable eyestrain, it turned into something I didn't quite recognize, something I'm even a little proud of.

I'd like to dedicate it to anyone who feels like the world wants less of them than there is.

BLOOD BENEATH THE SAND

MY FINGERS STUNG. It was an ingrained reaction, a holdover from when the instructors at the arcanum would rap my knuckles if I mislaid an equation. It happened every time the specifics of a formula began to puzzle me, which was more and more often these days. In my defense, this was a particularly complicated undertaking, and of course, I was carving the symbols into my forearm.

Blood ran in long rivulets down into the crook of my elbow as I reached the fifth permutation. It was a 3rd-rate formula, which meant 243 distinct variations before I could bring it 'round again, and time was running short.

The great double doors shuddered on their hinges, groaning under the impact of a dozen heavy battleaxes.

Blood Beneath the Sand

The men beside me waited with swords drawn, ink-black armor shimmering a dull gray in the firelight. Nobody spoke, but I could feel their eyes upon me as surely as the letters of a dead language slicing their way into my flesh. Just like me to leave my quill pens with the baggage train.

Blood began dripping onto the floor as I composed another verse of the conclusion. My phrasing was getting a tad derivative. You'd be surprised how efficient your prose becomes when each letter costs a thimble's worth of blood.

"Steady on, Devlin." That was Brick, a tall, bearded guy from the forests of northern Skara, trying his best to be comforting like usual, falling flat on his face like always.

I reached the end of the formula and anchored it by forcing the dagger point straight down to the bone. Nearly knocked myself clean out in the bargain. What an end that would have been for Devlin Narre.

A splintering crack, like a hundred year old tree hitting the ground, lashed through the hall as a long-axe cleft the doors in twain. Some overeager bastard stuck his head through the gap and got a mouthful of crossbow bolts for his trouble. Must've been greener than the day is long. No veteran trooper volunteers for anything without a dagger to his back.

I wiped the blood from my arm. It was the most gut-churning thing I'd done all day, running my hand along all those strips of flesh like the skin of a holiday roast. Began the wretched process of checking my work just the same though. As bad as being hacked to pieces by a gang of Uhlman raiders might sound, I assure you, spellcraft gone wrong can be worse.

I pursed my lips and studied the grisly characters as our boys worked through the last of their ammunition. "Forgot to carry the two." I muttered, and everyone groaned.

A spray of blood and spittle clipped me across the face as Brick cut down the first swordsman to make it through the door. Probably should've been standing further back from the breach. Whoops.

"Got it!" I shouted, just as Brick took a scimitar to the chestplate.

"Congratu-fuckin'-lations," he muttered, as the air came wheezing back into his lungs. "Care to lift us out of this damned mess, Lurk?"

Lurk was a name the boys had given me, back when magic used to spook them some. Brick didn't tend to use it. I must've been getting on his nerves.

"Heh ... yeah." I had the basic courtesy to look chagrined as company boys started wading into the melee.

I ran my hand over the bloody formula, watching it disappear from my arm as I did so. The pain didn't go, but I felt the power working through me just the same. Better than any drug this side of Jel-Nar, that feeling. You can see why the Sultan of Ruh and all his cronies got so addicted. Not me though, I always had too much fear in my heart to fall in love with it. Guess that's why I'm such a fourth-rate sorcerer.

I held the power inside me for barely a second before I sent it out into the aether like a kid hucking a sack-ball, hoping it would go through the goal posts without hitting anything important. This one did, and without much time to spare.

One of the Uhlmans, a big sergeant-looking type, hauled off and sent a javelin winging through the air straight at me. Brick tried to get his shield up, but I wouldn't blame him if he didn't try too hard. There was a sizzling sound like fire arrows stuck deep in a pikeman's ass as the spell took effect. The curved swords of the desert raiders teetered on their hilts for a heartbeat, before collapsing into reddish dust. The gleaming point of the javelin crumbled to powder a split second before the weighted haft belted me in the forehead.

I remember going down. You usually don't, but I remember the slow teetering and the fall, remember watching company guys wade into the Uhlman ranks wielding bronze-bladed weapons looted from the Emir's private collection. Maybe you think our boys took it easy on them, their not being armed and all. Maybe you don't know what it's like fighting street to street in the desert sun, buying your washed-up old wizard time to dot his i's and j's.

Anyway, there was a whole lot of red before things finally faded out black.

• • •

I woke up three minutes later. Doesn't sound like a lot, but trust me, it's long enough to slap the sense right out of you. A few more knocks like that and the screws would start coming loose for good. Hell, maybe they already had.

I sat up and yakked the contents of my stomach out onto the tiled floor. If that was the worst desecration the Emir's hall suffered today, we were worth more than he was paying us. I'll skip the blood and the guts and the screaming, but rest assured, there were plenty of all three to go around.

It was almost nightfall when I woke up the second time. I hadn't been unconscious; the day just winked past me, same way the hours slip by when you're asleep. Take enough stiff cracks to the head and it'll start happening to you too. Sometimes I'd slide into bed not knowing how I got there or when. Other times I'd sit down for chow, only to realize the food was gone and the barracks was empty.

This time, I looked around and found myself in the Emir's bedchamber. The Captain was there. Guess she and the Emir had relieved us in time. That was the handy thing about mercenary work. You can usually piece the broad strokes together, even if you weren't there for the particulars.

I was halfway ready to zone out again, when I glanced down and saw blood on the sheets. Took me longer than it should have to figure out whose it was.

"Fuck." Regular wordsmith, me. All the dead language poetry I'd read, and that was the best I could manage. "Fuck damn." Much better.

The Captain looked sideways at me. "Are you sober?"

"I won't make a habit of it."

"Hm." It was the closest the Captain ever came to laughter. "You just had one of your episodes, didn't you?"

"Yeah."

"You need filling in?"

"Probably."

She let out a long sigh and looked down at the blood-smeared satin. The light streaming in from the window was sallow and gray as stagnant water. It was enough to make even the luxury of the royal bedchamber feel empty. When the Captain looked back at me, her eyes were burning with hatred.

I didn't take that personal. The Captain hated everyone.

Every man in the company had their theory as to why. She was not a young woman, probably pushing fifty, plenty of time to wrong and be wronged by a world that didn't much care about her. Suppose I could've asked, but then, I *could* have walked out into the desert wearing nothing but my birthday suit. Somehow the urge never struck me.

"You recognize that?" She tilted her head toward the bed, or rather, what was lying in it.

I didn't want to take a second look, but some instincts are useless to fight. The thing was a corpse, that much was clear, but details were difficult to discern amidst its unnerving state of decay. The skin was mottled purple, with a gelatinous sheen that clung to the sheets where it rested. The hair and eyes had melted down into its skull, giving it the look of wet clay yet to be molded. The air had long been filled with the over-ripe stench of rotting flesh.

There was scarcely enough left of the body to determine the poor sod's gender, but the clothes it was wearing, along with its unlikely location, gave me sense enough what was happening.

"It's our employer." It felt like a kick in the stomach to say so, but it could only be the Emir of Al-Hasif, heir apparent to the Sultanate of Ruh, lying dead in his own juices before me. I glanced back at the Captain. It was only us two in the room. "Wasn't our doing was it?"

She gave me a hostile look ... that is to say, *particularly* hostile. "The company does not go back on a contract."

I shrugged and left the truth of that on the table. "Any idea how it happened?"

"A vague one." She produced a curved dagger from her waistband. "We found the business end stuck halfway into his back, minutes after the Uhlmans quit the field. You smell what I smell?"

I nodded. It smelled like an inside job. If the Uhlmans had a thing like that lined up, they would have done it before their army was driven off.

"Take a look."

I did. Beneath the flecks of clotted blood, the dagger was engraved with runic symbols, sorcerous symbols. I held the blade alongside my forearm, where the mottled scars of last morning's spellcraft had settled in amidst a backdrop of mangled flesh. The language on the dagger didn't match the signature of my own calculations. The prose was more florid, the arithmetic less halting. "It's old magic, the kind my instructors would have slapped me upside the head for even asking about."

"What can you make of it?"

I shrugged. "Tough to parse. I think whoever did this wanted to get inside the Emir's head. I've heard of weapons that can steal memories from the mind that holds them. These inscriptions fit the bill."

"And the state of the body?"

"This kind of thing doesn't tend to be gentle."

The Captain grunted.

"What else do we know?"

She waved a hand. "Bits and pieces. His guards reported seeing him less than an hour ago."

"There were bystanders?"

"*Were*." She smiled her hateful smile.

My stomach did a little backflip. She'd been right to do it, of course. If anyone found out the Emir had died in our care, the Captain's head would be first on the block, followed by the rest of ours. Suppose I was just going soft. "We need to get out while the getting's good."

"That would make us look guilty."

"We already look guilty."

She shrugged acknowledgement. "We'd never make the border; the Sultan's wizards would hunt us down like foxes."

I let out a long, dry breath. "So what do you need me for?"

"Simple." Her cold eyes flashed with spiteful humor. "Find the culprit."

I felt my eyebrows go up. "How do you know I didn't do it?"

"You're not a killer, Lurk."

"Wanna bet?"

She shook her head. "Not *this* kind of killer. You don't have the stomach for it." She said that as if it were a grievous fault I had as yet neglected to remedy. "Besides, you're my wizard. You deal with wizard shit. This sure as all hell smells the part."

The Captain always left the room when she was satisfied, regardless of if her counterpart felt the same. She made to do so now, but I caught her short with a question. "Do you think someone in the company did this?"

She opened the door a hair and looked at me. "No one else had the chance, Lurk … no one else has the nerve."

"Finding them won't get us out of this mess."

"Do your job," she said, already stepping into the hallway. "I'll do mine."

• • •

The scarlet sands danced with the whispering chaos of untapped magic. It was a thing scarcely noticed by the common soldiers who crossed it, but the deserts south of the Orin sea were alive with a spark of mischief. It was a land still watched over by the magic of an older time, by forces of wind and rain and desert sand not yet trampled beneath the march of roads and empires. From atop the narrow height of the citadel's tallest spire, I felt the distant thrum of that lingering presence, the way I'd imagine a shark feels the sun.

The streets below were alive with a hundred motes of light, lanterns strung across the rooftops to celebrate the Emir's return. I probably shouldn't have found that as amusing as I did, but when you live the merc's life, you take your yucks where you can get them, usually at someone else's expense.

I didn't know much about tracking down killers, but I did know a thing or two about magical goo-gaws, and this dagger had started to intrigue me. While the runes were familiar enough, the prose was in a language I didn't speak, an ancient desert tongue, dead to all but those who kept it alive for sordid purposes. There was nothing I could learn from the incantation itself, not without a laboratory and two sleepless months, but there was one symbol I could use.

The dagger had a smithy's mark, not a magical symbol, just a regular old signature. It meant the culprit had bought the weapon from a blacksmith before going on to make a magical marvel out of it. If I was lucky, that smithy was in the city and would have some information for sale.

I withdrew a thin scroll of parchment from my robe. The spell printed thereon was a 2nd-rate formula, three permutations, about as simple as they came.

I released the spell without much of the usual fanfare. I was too hot and dry and burnt out at both ends to take much pride in my work, and it wasn't much work besides. The symbol on the dagger, a pair of smithing hammers curled around one another, began to emit a deep, fire-red glow. Looking out across the city, I saw a larger version of the same symbol, blaring away in the darkness.

• • •

The blacksmith's shop was a small, ramshackle kind of place, which probably meant they were good. A well-kept smithy meant gilded pommels and ruby cross guards and all the other things that get looted from your corpse when an ugly blade busts your pretty one to pieces.

I went in and asked for the head smith. He was a short, tan-skinned guy with the kind of shoulders you'd expect to get from swinging a hammer around all your life. He muttered and spat on the ground when he saw me. "You're back."

That brought me up short for a second. "We know each other?"

"Not as dance partners. Saw you in here two nights ago."

I blinked. "Sorry, my head's a little screwy just lately, took a hard knock off the top. You know how it goes."

He grunted.

"You mind filling me in on just what I was doing here?"

The guy gave me a suspicious look, like he thought he was being conned but couldn't settle on how. Eventually, he shrugged. "You walked in, asked for a dagger done up in the old fashion. Good, clean steel, you said. No impurities, no folding. Figured you might be drunk or some such, the way your eyes were all glazed-over like."

"I see." Pure steel would be easier to carve an incantation into, no lingering faults to mess with the characters. For a split second, I thought maybe I *had* killed the Emir. "Don't suppose I mentioned what it was for?"

His eyes narrowed and he spat on the soot-covered ground once more. "No, I don't suppose you did."

"Thanks anyway." I said, and got out of there as fast as wobbly legs would take me, which didn't end up being very fast, seeing how my head was spinning like a top.

Not just spinning, as it happened. I was going out again, going under, and this time, I had some idea what it meant.

I slapped myself twice across the face and stumbled into an alleyway. I couldn't fight the sudden fatigue that was stalking my mind like a predator, but I might be able to do something about it before I went.

I placed a hand on the wall as the alleyway began to spin and fumbled a quill pen from my satchel. I began searching for the inkwell as my body was wracked with feverish shivers.

Fuck it.

Blood spurted across my face as I jammed the quill into my wrist. I started writing on the sandstone wall before me. My connection with the waking world was becoming more theoretical by the moment, but the pain in my wrist kept me lucid. When everything else had faded into half-remembered nothing, I clung to the pain like a lifeline. I didn't know if I'd finished the spell, didn't know if it would rip me to pieces when I cast it, but I ran a crimson hand along the blood-smeared wall just the same.

There was a sound like rushing air, and my shoulder crunched against the paving stones. I felt a subtle warmth in my chest and cast what there was to be cast.

There was a shout and a crash and everything went quiet.

• • •

I was on my feet when I awoke. That sent a jolt of panic right down to my toes. I started wondering how long I'd been out, what the hell I had done in the meantime, but it didn't take me too long to realize I was still in the alleyway. Nothing happened when I tried to move my head, nor when I tried to stem the blood flowing out of my wrist.

I felt my neck crane downward slowly, but it wasn't me who did the craning. Something ... *else* was controlling me. Something else inspected my blood-soaked forearm and lowered a sleeve to conceal it.

The spell had worked.

Whatever force had been compelling me to action during my blackouts was still in control, but this time I was lucid; this time I would *see* what exactly I was being used to achieve.

Maybe you're wondering why I didn't just shut the thing out of my head entirely. Well, you see, I had this crazy notion that I'd uncover the plot from the inside, learn what this thing had done with me, and keep it feeling comfortable right up until the axe came down.

Yeah.

If you're thinking it's a pisspoor state of affairs when Devlin Narre starts playing hero, I wish you'd been around at the time.

• • •

Brick called out a challenge when the thing that was not quite me stumbled back into the Emir's palace. My body held up a bloody hand in greeting and walked on. The big man raised an eyebrow as I passed. "Where you been skulking about?"

"Your mother's bedchamber."

Thing didn't do a half bad me, actually.

He rolled his eyes past the snickering. "Yeah, whatever, Lurk." Guess I could stop wondering why his patience had been running short lately. I saw him look away and look back in a hurry. "Fuck me sideways! You're bleeding like a spigot!"

"Reel your neck in," I heard myself snarl.

"Reel my-- did you fall off your fucking high horse? What the hell's been the matter with you?"

The thing controlling me turned sharply, and I found myself facing down every corn-fed, blue-eyed inch of him. There must have been something dangerous in my expression, because he took an uneasy step back. "You wanna be a big man and find out?" I asked.

After three heartbeats of silence, I turned on a dime and marched off, feeling Brick's eyes on the back of my skull all the while.

Blood Beneath the Sand

• • •

The thing ended up leading me downward, down through the servant's quarters, down through the dungeon, down through a blocked off section of wall that no one, not even company sappers, would have found in a lifetime spent looking.

The stairs grew damp and slippery as the memory of illumination faded, and the air began to reek with the closeness of rotting plants. I wouldn't have seen an elephant three steps ahead of me in the darkness, but the thing inside me knew where it was going.

Eventually, after what must have been a mile's descent, the stairs gave way to cold, soft earth. Plants and gripping vines, the likes of which had no place amidst the desert sands, clutched at my face as I marched through the perfect blackness. I stepped into something wet and clutching, like the rolling bogs back home, and sank right up to my knees.

Down here, in the aging bowels of a chasm forgotten by time, the air should have sat close and heavy as a stagnant pool, but as I waited, boots soiling in the muck, I felt a warm breeze snicker through my hair.

The thing that was almost me reached into its pocket and gripped the cold hilt of a runic dagger, the Emir's blood scarcely dry on its blade. The force inside my head did something I was not quite prepared for then ... it *thought.*

If you don't know what it feels like to have something else thinking inside your head, at least you'll always have that.

I learned a few things then. I learned that the being controlling me was a rival which time and death had come up against and failed, I learned that the presence of so many feckless wizards in a desert made quiet by its slumber had roused a primal anger from the unthinking darkness of its lair, and I learned the purpose of the dagger, proffered in my grasp like a talisman.

I learned and wished I could unlearn. Wished I could … if nothing else … scream.

I felt something reach out to grasp the blade, something wet and dexterous and slow. My spine didn't go rigid. My legs didn't wobble. The thing that wasn't me faced this ancient terror with all the steadiness of the grave, and that was most terrifying of all.

The dagger was lifted from my grasp, and in that moment, I learned what knowledge it contained, what secrets were so hidden in the Emir's memory that even this primordial mind had resorted to theft and murder to obtain them.

Names.

Not given names.

Names older and truer than the men and women who bore them.

The true names of every one of the Sultan's fearsome cabal, knowledge entrusted only to the monarch and his immediate family, knowledge that, if wielded with ill-intent, would bring a country and a people shuddering helplessly to their knees.

The creature whose thoughts were mine and not mine turned those names over in its mind and was pleased.

As I was steered back through the wet, clinging jungle of a land forgotten by time, I felt suddenly cold and helpless and very, very small.

• • •

The thing had not spelled out what it intended to do with all those names, but it didn't take a degree from the arcanum to realize it had plans for the company.

The Sultan commanded one of the most feared arcane cabals in the world, men and women single-handedly responsible for the pathetic state of this country's military. What need for pikes and arrows and lances when no foreign power would dare meet your arcanists on the field?

With that lot out of the picture, a core of hard fighting men could march the length of this desert and back again and never meet a force that could stop them. Our six hundred company men could rid this desert of all the troublesome gnats who dared disturb the tranquility with their spellcraft.

With every step up the moss-covered stairway, I willed my feet to stop their inexorable journey. I fought desperately against the force controlling my body because, without the Captain, I was first in line to inherit command. Without the Captain, this *thing* would hold the fate of all my brothers and sisters in its palm. Without the Captain, all was lost, and I knew I was going to kill her.

• • •

The halls were empty as the thing that was not quite me shambled its way through the palace, casting long, uneven shadows across the floor. I tried clenching my fists, slowing my stride, anything to regain some kind of control. Nothing worked.

I was all but resigned to my fate, when Brick stepped out from the shadows. Big, dumb, innocent Brick, massive arms folded across his chest. "Where the hell have you been?"

My body tried to walk around him. I prayed to every god that he would let that stand, but he didn't, of course he didn't.

A hand shot out and grabbed me by the collar, shoving me back into the wall. "You slimy bastard, *answer me!*" He all but lifted me off the ground in his grasp. "I saw you go down into them dungeons, didn't come back up for hours. What the fuck do you think you're up to?"

"This isn't a fight you want to pick." I could feel my hands clenching into fists, could feel the well of arcane power welling up inside me. I didn't have time to prepare a spell, but I had rainy day magic to spare, some of which I would have been ashamed to use against a common soldier. I didn't think the force in my head had any such convictions.

I probably don't need to tell you that Brick didn't walk away. He wasn't that kind of guy. I heard a shout from down the corridor and turned to see half a dozen company men moving toward us, drawn to the sound of our arguing.

I felt the terrible heat of arcane fire rising in my chest as an anger that was not my own wrapped its hands around my throat. Nothing I had done to combat the force controlling me had worked thus far, I doubted anything would, but even so, I tried to fight it.

I need you to believe I tried.

• • •

The effort must have blacked me out because I woke up to a smell like rotten eggs and burning charcoal. It was the sulphuric, flash-lightning scent of war magic recently cast. I looked down and saw a vision straight out of a waking nightmare.

Brick was on the ground, what was left of him anyway. Fire and arcane force had hardened his flesh like the skin of a suckling pig, melting the links of his heavy chain shirt into a twisted mesh of iron and blood. He stared up at the ceiling with the empty, slack-jawed look of a man not expecting to die.

The vaunted hallway had been torn apart by fire and acid and god knew what other kind of magical terror. A wasp the size of a small dog was feasting on the corpse of a man in company uniform. I felt a familiar twinge of pain in my knuckles and knew that I had done it.

I heard the thrum of racing footsteps as I collapsed to my knees in the blood.

I collapsed to my knees.

The thing controlling me must have burned through the time or the energy or the will necessary to maintain its hold. I wondered if Brick would have been satisfied, knowing his death had saved the company. I wondered if it mattered.

"Lurk." I looked up to find the Captain staring at me like a wounded animal that needed to be put down. Behind her stood twenty battle-hardened veterans whose eyes were nonetheless filled with the light of primal terror. "What the hell happened here?"

I glanced down at my hands and made a helpless gesture with arms that scarcely obeyed. "I found the killer."

• • •

Evan Davies

The floor of my cell was wet with seeping groundwater. Suppose that might have been a clue to the thing lurking below, but right now, I was more concerned with how the trousers clung to my ass cheeks. I wanted to scratch, but my hands were sealed inside a cylinder of tailored steel, preventing even my fingers from twitching.

I sat up as a pair of shadows trickled in through the rusted bars. One was a woman, tall and slender, with the coal-smeared eyes of a desert sorceress. I hadn't bothered to learn her given name. She was only there to prevent my escape.

The other was the Captain.

"You have five minutes," the sorceress muttered, before stalking back down the corridor. She would be listening, I knew, no matter how far she appeared to stray.

The Captain folded her arms and looked down at me. It must have been quite the pitiful sight. They'd stripped me of my robe and all its contents, leaving only an undershirt against the damp. For all that, there was no hatred in her eyes this time. I found that uniquely strange.

"They wanted to draw and quarter you," she said, at last. "I talked them down to beheading."

"My hero." There was less sarcasm in my voice than you'd think.

She sighed again and rubbed her eyes. "Lurk ... Devlin ... What is this? What aren't you telling me?"

"What makes you think there's more to be told?"

"Oh fuck off." She folded her arms. "I'd buy that shit from anyone else, but not you. Why the Emir? Why *Brick*?"

I grimaced and sat forward. "Brick just ... got in the way."

"Of what?" she asked. I glanced down the corridor, where the sorceress had disappeared. The Captain followed my gaze. "Ah."

I nodded. "There's nothing to be gained by telling you. That's the truth. If the Emir's generals will let you go, you should go."

The Captain kept her gaze pointed down the hall for some moments. Eventually she lowered herself to the ground, sitting cross-legged on the dampened stonework. "Is that what you want?"

I nodded again. "Get out of the city, out of the country. Don't look back until you reach the Jin-Haran mountains, and keep on marching even then."

She gave me an uncertain look. "I'll get you out of here if you give me a reason."

I chuckled, a little sadly. Never paid much mind to eavesdroppers, our Captain. "Can I ask you something?"

She waved me onward.

"What do we owe each other?" I asked.

"You and me?"

"The company, brothers in arms, anyone who sells their blood for silver. We live our lives in the shadow of men and women made larger by the weight of the coin in their pocket ... or the magic in their archives. We do horrible things, suffer horrible injustices. It seems to me there's no bond we won't sever, no faith we won't betray, to steal one more day from the gods, so I'm asking, what do we owe each other, if we don't owe the world a damn thing?"

Maybe that seems like senseless rambling to you, maybe that's all it was, but the Captain understood; life hadn't allowed her not to. The answer was simple and unyielding as the hard-bitten woman who gave it. "Everything."

I looked down at my steel-clad hands and nodded. "That's why I can't tell you what happened here. I owe it to my brothers to get what's left of the company out of this place. I owe it to Brick to do something on my own. If you knew what that was, you'd help me, and the company's gonna need you alive."

She grabbed hold of her ankles and leaned back slowly, watching me with the steady gaze of a hunter. There was a word for why I couldn't tell her the truth, for why she would have stood by me if I did.

The Captain lived in a world that thought honor was just another way to scream foul play when the other guy's gotten the better of you. It was why she hated so much and so freely. I fancied it was why, in this moment at least, she stopped just short of hating me, but that was probably wishful thinking.

She stayed with me, down there in the darkness, as our five minutes ticked gently past. She was waiting for something she knew I wouldn't give her, but she waited just the same.

When the door at the end of the hall swung open, she rose from the ground and walked out.

• • •

There's no easy way to tell time when you're locked in perfect darkness. I figured it would take the company about a day to shoulder pack and put a good few miles between them and Al-Hasif. 24 hours, 86,400 seconds. I counted them all. I was a soldier. Drudgery was a way of life.

The count was nearing its end when torchlight swept through the catacombs once more. The sorceress had returned, backed by two grim-looking warriors.

"Rise," she said.

I rose.

"You will answer to the high tribunal for your crimes."

"My company?"

I might've imagined the gloating smile on her lip. "They have abandoned you to a man."

I nodded slowly. "I guess we'd better get started then." I paused and took a long breath. I'd have to get this right the first time. "*Amiran Ashfaqin.*"

The woman's spine went suddenly rigid. It was not the name her parents had given her. It was a name written in the stars long before she was born. It was the secret, bottomless well from which all her power was drawn, and I had taken hold of it surely as if I had wrapped a hand around her throat.

I glanced at the uneasy guards to either side of her. "Remove them."

The two men barely had time to look surprised before their spears turned to pythons and strangled them. Maybe that was more than they deserved, but you try counting to 79,562 and see what kind of mood it leaves you in.

"Get me out of this fucking cell." She did, and after she'd removed the metal that bound my wrists, I flexed my fingers gratefully. "How many more of the Sultan's cabal are in the city?"

When she spoke, her voice was her own. She was still there, still thinking and acting for herself. She just couldn't do anything unless I willed it. A scary thing, being named. You can see why the Sultan's wizards stayed in line. "Three." She licked her lips nervously. "They flew in to oversee your execution."

I nodded at that. Killing a wizard, even a cut rate one like me, was a tricky proposition, full of opportunities for spite and parting revenge. "Can you call them here without arousing their suspicion?"

Her face turned pale. "Yes."

"Good." I said, rubbing my wrists. "We've got work to do."

• • •

A flame clicked to life in my hand as I watched the spiral staircase wind down into the bowels of the desert. Firelight cast the slime-covered walls in a dull, shifting gray, lessening the unease of the place slightly, if only slightly.

I turned around to face the four wizards arrayed behind me. The one set to guard me, Amiran, was the baby of the group at just over two hundred years old. The others had been given more time to augment their bodies for sorcerous effect. One of them, a hunched, bearded man with the touch of the desert in his skin, stared back at me with eyes of pure diamond. Another had a gnarled tree branch for an arm. The digits of its fingers crackled like dry kindling when she moved them.

They were the oldest, most powerful magi in a country scarcely known for much else, and despite all the indignant pride that came with such a fact, I don't think I imagined the pleading note in their expressions.

"If what you've told us is true." Amiran's voice was hesitant. "You're leading us all to our deaths."

"Maybe."

"Have you no compassion?" the old man hissed.

"For you?" I shrugged. "You've had a millennium between you to enjoy the power of gods and all the luxuries of an empire. I'd say it's well past time you earned your keep. What is all that power for if not to shelter the meek from forces like this?"

There were answers to that question, of course, but none, they correctly surmised, that would have been particularly persuasive to me.

"Anything else?" I asked.

Amiran sighed. "Your friend won't care one way or another if you die down there."

"This ain't about Brick."

"It won't redeem you for killing him."

"It's not about me, either."

"Then what the hell is it about?!" She spoke with the shrill panic of someone whose purpose in life was never to die.

I shook my head, not without sympathy. "We in the company don't have a lot, but each one of us who goes down, does it believing that the others won't let them go quietly. Someone takes a swing at our brothers, we take a swing right back, even if we're gonna miss, even if there's not much use in trying. Maybe that's hard for you to understand, but there's gotta be something in life you believe in more than yourself. Otherwise, you're just taking up space for a while. No one fights for us, so we fight for each other. I think that's as good a thing to die for as any."

There was silence for a long time, and I imagined I could feel the waiting creature's breath flowing in and out like the tide. Eventually, Amiran closed her eyes and looked away. "A lifetime learning your craft and all you have to show for it is a reason to die."

I gave a half-hearted smile and thought of all the dead men whose names I'd forgotten. "That's more than most people get," I said, and began the long climb down to the thing that waited below.

ABOUT THE AUTHOR

Evan Davies bounced between the United States and Canada for a number of years before the pandemic put an abrupt stop to that. The many, many lockdowns provided him with a unique opportunity to focus on his writing career.

Since then, he has published a number of short stories, all with a penchant for genre-mashing and tonal incongruity. He is currently working on a full-length novel.

In his free time, Evan is an avid reader, road-tripper, table-top gamer, amateur boxer, and *jiu-jitsu* practitioner.

His only particular goal in life is to make enough money writing so that he doesn't have to hold down a real job.

YOU MIGHT ALSO ENJOY

THE ALCHEMIST DAUGHTER
by Paul S. Moore

When a concoction of ethers channels a little of their magic properties to one location, inspiration springs to life.

GREY MOTHER MOUNTAIN
by Elyse Russell

When her village is destroyed, an elderly woman seeks help from the last remaining dragon to get revenge.

THE INN OF THE SEVEN STARS
by Kevin Beckett

A tale of an inn with good music, tasty food, strong beer ... and inadvertent necromancy.

Available in digital and trade paperback editions from
Water Dragon Publishing
waterdragonpublishing.com

www.ingramcontent.com/pod-product-compliance
Lightning Source LLC
LaVergne TN
LVHW040203080526
838202LV00042B/3312